The Old Man and
His Xylophone
Onyinye Udeh

Onyinye Udeh

The Old Man and His Xylophone

Onyinye Udeh

Pearly Gates Publishing LLC
INSPIRING CHRISTIAN AUTHORS TO BE AUTHORS

Pearly Gates Publishing, LLC, Houston, Texas

The Old Man and His Xylophone

The Old Man and His Xylophone

ISBN13: 9798734622865
Amazon Assigned - Independently Published

Disclaimer: The following story is a work of fiction. Names, characters, businesses, places, events, locales, and incidents are either the products of the author's imagination or used in a fictitious manner. Any resemblance to actual persons, living or dead, or actual events is purely coincidental.

Editing, Typesetting, and Publishing:
Pearly Gates Publishing, LLC
Angela Edwards, CEO
P.O. Box 62287
Houston, TX 77205
BestSeller@PearlyGatesPublishing.com

Dedication

This book is dedicated to my late, loving father,

Mr. Abel O. Ogbonna.

Having him in my life was such a huge blessing. He was a great storyteller who inspired me to become the author and storyteller I am today.

Acknowledgments

To the love of my life, my darling husband, Edwin Udeh: You have been my driving force and a great support in every way. Thank you.

To my beloved beautiful children—Greatness Udeh, Amarachukwu Udeh, and Royalty Udeh: You are the greatest gift of God to me. Words cannot express how much I love you. You are the reason for my relentless efforts. Having you in my life has inspired me in so many ways.

To my brother, Vincent Ogbonna: You inspired me to write this story. I appreciate you for your support and prayers. Thank you.

To my beautiful, sweet mother: I appreciate you. I am proud to be your daughter, mama. You are my teacher and role model. Thank you for all your support and for standing by me up to this day.

To my wonderful siblings—Chisom, Otuto, and Ekeoma Ogbonna, Ngozi Onwo, and Lovina Nwobodo (Mrs.): You have stood by me all my life. Thank you for your prayers and love towards me. I appreciate you.

To all the late Richard Udeh families: Thank you all. You are such a wonderful family.

To that great Woman of God, Prophetess Catherine Agbango: Getting to know you is such a huge blessing. Thank you for your spiritual support and guidance.

To my pastor, Pastor Sunny Lawani, and his beautiful wife, Pastor Mrs. Clementina Lawani: Thank you for your spiritual support. Being with you has added so much to my life.

Introduction

This is the story of Mazi Ogom Iloha and his unmatched love for both his xylophone and youngest son.

Both brought forth joy and pain to his life.

Both were irreplaceable…

Table of Contents

The Story...

Mazi Ogom Iloha was a man blessed with three sons and no daughter. In most African countries, fathering boys is a blessing and deeply appreciated. For instance, instead of having numerous female children in a household, an African man would rather have only one male child. Female children are valued, but not as much in comparison to the males, for the fear exists that they will end up belonging to another family or perhaps marrying someone from a different race, thereby breaking their family's heart and leaving them deserted. That is common in African homes where there is no male child. Ideally, the blessing of a male child will carry on the family's name.

As for Mazi Iloha, although his home was filled with only boys, things were not quite as they should have been. From the outside looking in, one would have expected him to be joyful with all his sons—and anyone thinking along those lines would have guessed incorrectly. There was something about his youngest son, Ikem, that limited his joy…something he wanted to conceal from every outsider's eye. However, it seemed like the more he tried to hide it, the more problematic the cover-up became.

Author's Note: *My people often say, "Life is not complete for anyone in this world." There's always something — a constant reminder that we're visitors in this world.*

The situation concerning Ikem had gotten to the point that Mazi's other two sons often felt cheated. To them, it appeared obvious their father had chosen their younger brother over them. While it may have appeared that was the case, the actual reason for favoritism went much deeper. There was so much more to the story.

As a result of the attention Mazi Iloha gave Ikem, it looked like the position of power that was promised to the eldest son, Nwude, was slowly but surely being handed over to his youngest brother. Was the culture subjected to a change of which he was not aware? Nwude was perplexed. *Who wouldn't be when forced to fight for your position constantly?* He tried his hardest to present himself to his father as capable of adhering to tradition and make him realize that he, too, was hungry for his father's love, especially since there was the absence of their mother to contend with.

Mazi Iloha was a farmer, but most of his earnings were made through his unique gift: making melodious music with his xylophone. Many would simply refer to him as "The Xylophone Player." He had a rare talent at the time, as most people did not know how to play or even build a xylophone. So, anytime there was a special occasion such as a funeral or festival, people would gather in great numbers just to listen and dance to the tunes and rhythms of that great man.

Mazi Iloha was extremely popular among his people for his craft of playing the musical instrument. He never spoke a word while playing, but his countenance each time spoke loudly. One could never begin to guess what was on his mind, yet he always seemed like a man driven by sorrow. He would appear to be in a trance while playing the xylophone as if he were off in a faraway land, yet he never played a wrong note.

One would think his musical gift was his first love, were it not for the fact that life's difficulties made themselves known to him. As a man full of knowledge and understanding about life, he understood quite well and never blamed anyone for the challenges that were presented, even in his own family.

One occasion arose when he could not help but outwardly show the preference he had for Ikem. On Iriji Day — the New Yam Festival, which was one of their land's greatest traditions — a problem surfaced. During Iriji in Umoji town, each family was tasked with having something alive to offer for the ceremonial slaughter. Typically, that day was joyful as the people celebrated and were merry. On that particular day, though, the day turned into something rather unpleasant.

When the goat for the ceremony was presented to be slaughtered on behalf of Mazi Iloha's family, instead of offering the honor to his eldest son, he gave the assignment to Ikem. Mazi Iloha was very intentional with his decision. He planned to keep Ikem busy and restrain him from leaving the compound that day. Instead of it working out the way he had planned, trouble arose, and feelings were hurt. He was a man with a gentle nature — never meaning to hurt anyone's feelings—but that day, he did.

After being slighted to what he believed was the highest degree, Nwude got angry and swiftly stormed out of the compound, despite his father's request to come back to the festivities. Nwude's absence was noticeable and had ruined his family's day because it was evident that something had, indeed, gone wrong. Later that evening, he returned when he thought everyone had retired to bed for the night—but the old man had remained awake, waiting for him.

Nwude tried to sneak in quietly and avoid doing anything that would awaken those sleeping. Just as he was about to lay down, his father's voice floating through the darkness of the night startled him.

"Welcome home, son," the elderly man gently greeted as he turned on the light.

"Oh! Papa, are you still awake?" Nwude hastily asked as he turned in the direction of the voice.

"Yes, my son. I have been waiting for you. I am glad you are back safely."

"I am sorry, Papa. I overreacted."

"You have done nothing wrong, my son. Still, I am not happy that you did not get to join your family."

"I have things to deal with, Papa," Nwude replied with an audible sigh.

"Not by leaving the way you did, son." Nwude then apologized again. Mazi Iloha continued, "Nwude, you are my son—my firstborn. From the moment you were born, I have had a special love for you. This very night, I want you to know that nobody can take your place in my heart. Your coming has only brought me good tidings, never heartache. Time and time again, you have proven yourself worthy of being the first child. I love each of you with the same measure of love, but let's be realistic here: You and Ekene are both healthy and able to take care of yourselves. But Ikem? I have great concern for him." He then reached out his arms toward his son, beckoned to him, and said, "Come, my son. Sit opposite of me."

Nwude relaxed his defensive posture and followed his father's gentle, loving guidance to have a seat.

"Your brother is a sick child, Nwude." He noticed his son raise a questioning eyebrow. "No, he is not physically ill, but he is troubled. I suppose he has had that ill fate ever since his birth. Your mother died a few hours after giving birth to him, so he was never afforded the opportunity to be breastfed like you and Ekene. Ikem only had goat's milk when he was a baby. You remember, don't you?"

Nwude nods and recalls the days of their youth as a look of sadness comes over his face.

"Nwanne gi nwoke n'eme aka ntutu o bu ogafere otuturu. Ikem is a thief!" the old man exclaimed. "That, my son, is his illness. He falls for any little temptation. His thievery is more than a disease. He doesn't know when he does it. He cries and lives with the shame. I have watched you and your brother cry with him and try to protect him anytime he is paraded through the village with the items he stole hanging around his neck. It brings shame not only to him but to us as well! I will go to any length to see that it stops! Do you now understand why it seems like I love him more than anyone?"

Nwude nodded again, indicating to his father that, yes, he understood.

Mazi Iloha went on. "Well, I do not love him more than you or your brother. I do, however, pity him. It hurts deep in my heart when I see the pain, hopelessness, and despair in his eyes. I believe that by keeping him busy and close to me, he will be distracted. Perhaps you now see why I watch him all the time like a hawk that watches a chicken. Anytime someone states they have something missing, my heart is always rent in pieces." He swallowed hard before continuing, thinking carefully about his next words. "I want you and Ekene to support me. I am older now and physically ill. Although I do not always feel the best, I know there are some conditions that are worse in others. I will not have my rest until Ikem is freed from his thievery curse!"

Alas, Ikem was, indeed, freed, but it was not the kind of freedom for which his father had hoped…

Mazi Iloha vowed to do all he could to help his son stop stealing, but his efforts proved ineffective. It seemed the more he tried, the more his son became even more criminally-minded. He had little regard for his father's words. One day, he would promise to stop; the next, he would strike again. All the while, he was growing from a young lad who stole chickens and eggs from the villagers, to a full-blown, hardcore, and notorious criminal. While others his age had full-time and respectable responsibilities, Ikem had moved out of his father's house and, at every turn, broke the law by robbing and killing. Not long after, he was declared wanted by the law…***dead or alive.***

Ikem's family cried and mourned for him, even while he was alive. Their comfort came by way of committing everything into the hands of the Creator. Meanwhile, they waited for the moment they knew would come eventually: the law would find him and strike. No one knew the day nor the hour, but they were sure it would come to pass.

Sure enough, it wasn't too long before Ikem was caught. The news about his capture spread far and wide, including in his village. Nwude and Ekene heard about their little brother's capture before their father and wanted to protect him from the bad news. After crying and consoling themselves, Nwude prepared himself to tell their father, but Ekene was hesitant.

"Not yet," Ekene said. He cried as he held tight to his brother's shirt, restraining him. "It will kill the old man."

"Would you rather he heard it from the villagers, Ekene? Sooner or later, the old man "will hear. I think it would be wise if we were the ones to break the news to him."

When they told Mazi Iloha about his son's capture, it did nearly kill him. The old man cried and refused to be consoled. At that moment, the three men cried together, comforted one another, and reminisced, even as they awaited the day of Ikem's execution by the firing squad.

Before that fateful day, Mazi Iloha and his sons went to visit Ikem in prison. He had always been a tough guy— hardened and without human emotions. That was the kind of man he grew up to become, and he didn't change—even when he knew he was about to die. He refused to meet with his family and, instead, sent a message through the guards that he wrote on a piece of paper:

"Tell the old man I am sorry. It is my wish that we part this way. All my life, I've caused him nothing but pain. Let him remember me as the nine-year-old Ikem— the one he used to carry on his lap. I guess

I am that one thing about life that he must always bear."

His final wish was granted.

"So long, my son. Ya diwa nwam," the old man gallantly said after the contents of the letter were read aloud.

Once again, father and sons cried with the heaviness of pain in their hearts. That was the last time Mazi Iloha had to spend with his son, yet he was denied the opportunity to bid him goodbye and hug him one last time. No matter what Ikem had done, his father still loved him.

"Nothing has changed. He is still my son," he muttered softly to no one in particular.

Mazi Iloha and Ekene returned home, their hearts sorrowful, while Nwude stayed behind to witness his youngest brother's execution. His father sternly told him to return home as soon as the execution was over. It was a difficult decision to make, but Nwude had no choice. The more he thought about it, he saw it as a better way to deal with the pain. He knew he would forever live with remembering seeing his brother's face one last time, but also knew he needed the closure, leaving no room for regret.

When the time came, Nwude could not bring himself to watch Ikem being killed. He saw his brother from afar for a brief moment as they led him out. He wanted to scream his name, but the sound got stuck in his throat. Once the shooting started, he could not bear to hear his brother's painful cry and the cheers coming from the onlookers. That was when he took to his heels and ran far away. When he was out of view, he collapsed on the bare ground and cried uncontrollably.

It took him some time to recover from the horrific event. He found himself questioning if it was wrong of him to accept staying behind. In the end, he was no closer to achieving what he thought it would do. He only succeeded in engraving sorrow in his heart and an unforgettable image in his mind that would be hard to erase. Once he recovered from the ordeal and pulled himself together, he hurried home.

Upon entering the compound, he was met by his father and a group of the village's men. The entirety of other xylophone players stood with his father in support. It was apparent they were awaiting his return.

Shortly after, he fell into the arms of one of the men, shaking wildly with raw emotion. That prompted the men to react to the old man's command: "Take him inside. It is time to bid Ikem farewell."

As he began to play his xylophone, the music's sound tore through the atmosphere and changed the mood within the compound. It wasn't a pleasant tune, though. It was one filled with the sorrows of life, death, and the challenges people encounter in life that constantly reminded everyone they were strangers in this world. It told the story of his pain...his grief. The sound drew the villagers to surround him.

Ordinarily, many would not have come, yet as they assembled in great numbers, they cried along with Mazi Iloha and his sons. The strange way of mourning his son caused tears to fall from the faces of every man, woman, and child. Their hearts were heavy, which made them overlook the fact that his dead son had been a thief and murderer and, therefore, deserved his punishment. At that moment, the onlookers only saw a man in sorrow who grieved the loss of a son he loved.

Everyone knew Mazi Iloha's story and the pains both he and his family endured as Ikem was growing up. They remembered the times he was caught, beaten, stripped naked, and paraded around the whole village.

Nonetheless, the villagers mourned with Mazi Ogom Iloha as they shared in the unique moment he said his goodbyes to his son in the most beautiful, melodious way. It was his peculiar way of saying farewell to his son that birthed this story.

THE END

About the Author

Onyinye Udeh grew up in Enugu State in the Eastern part of Nigeria. She obtained a B.S. degree in Communication from Enugu State University of Science and Technology. She self-published a romance book titled "Love Without Flower" and also had a story she wrote titled "Nne The Jewel of Ukelu Kingdom" that was translated into a motion picture. The Executive Producer on that project was her husband, Edwin Udeh.

Onyinye presently resides in Texas (USA) with her husband and three beautiful children: Greatness, Darlene, and Royalty Udeh.

www.ingramcontent.com/pod-product-compliance
Lightning Source LLC
Chambersburg PA
CBHW060949130726
48001CB00003B/1125